BIGGETY BAT

Chow Down, Biggety!

by Ann Ingalls
Illustrated by Aaron Zenz

SCHOLASTIC INC.

To Msie from Annsie. Much love. —A.I.

This is for (Who could it be?)...Mercy, Eden, and Haven! — A.Z.

Text copyright © 2015 by Ann Ingalls
Cover and interior art copyright © 2015 by Aaron Zenz

All rights reserved. Published by Scholastic Inc., *Publishers since 1920*. SCHOLASTIC and associated logos are trademarks and/or registered trademarks of Scholastic Inc.

The publisher does not have any control over and does not assume any responsibility for author or third-party websites or their content.

This book is a work of fiction. Names, characters, places, and incidents are either the product of the author's imagination or are used fictitiously, and any resemblance to actual persons, living or dead, business establishments, events, or locales is entirely coincidental.

ISBN 978-0-545-66264-2

12 11 10 9 8 7 6 5 4 3 2 1   15 16 17 18 19/0

Printed in the U.S.A.   40
First printing, July 2015

Book design by Maria Mercado

As the moon shone on the salty sea,
Biggety Bat left his mangrove tree.

He went sniffing for some supper.

In the branches
Biggety Bat heard
someone snacking—

CRACK! CRACK!

Who could it be?

A CUCKOO!
Nibbling on grubs.

"**Hot diggety!**" said Biggety.
"Supper for cuckoo, but...
what about me?"

Below his tree
Biggety Bat heard
someone crunch—

MUNCH! MUNCH!

Who could it be?

LEOPARD FROG!

Feasting on bugs.

"**Hot diggety!**" said Biggety.
"Supper for frog, but . . .
what about me?"

In the water
Biggety Bat heard
someone swallow—

GLUG! GLUG!

Who could it be?

SPOONBILL!

Scooping up shrimp.

"Hot diggety!" said Biggety.
"Supper for spoonbill, but...
what about me?"

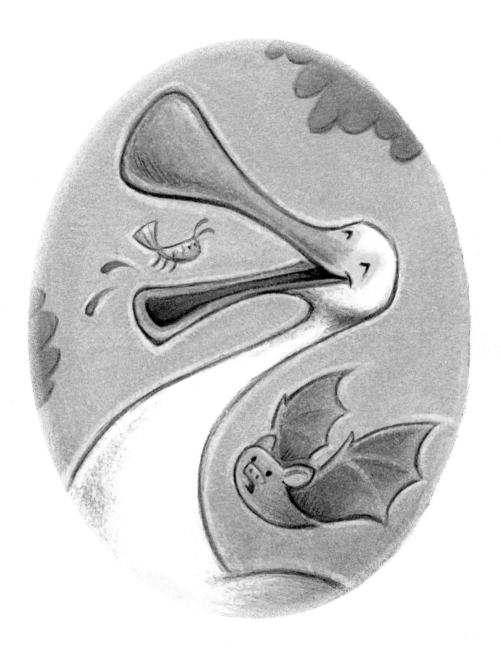

In the shadows
Biggety Bat heard
someone chew—

GREEN SEA TURTLE!

Grazing on grass.

"Hot diggety!" said Biggety.
"Supper for sea turtle, but...
what about me?"

Near the water
Biggety Bat heard
someone guzzle—

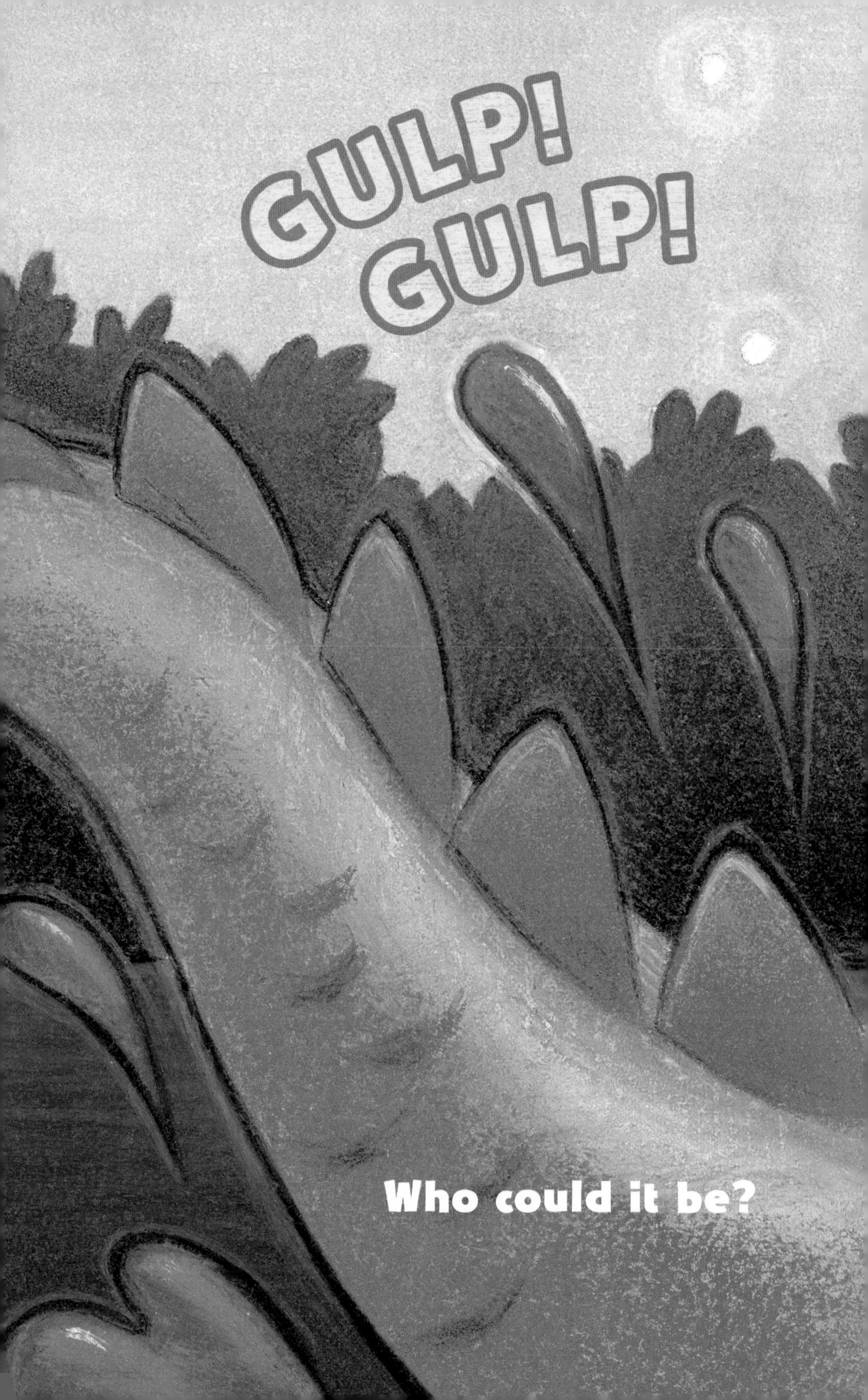

Who could it be?

ALLIGATOR!
Snapping up fish.

"*Hot diggety!*" said Biggety.
"Supper for alligator, but . . .
what about me?"

All around him
Biggety Bat heard
something hum—

Who could it be?

MOSQUITOES!

Biggety Bat tumbled and dove.

"Hot diggety!" said Biggety.
"Buzzing bugs! Supper for me."

A breeze blew through
the grove of trees.

This mangrove is the place to be!
"Hot diggety!" said Biggety.

A FLORIDA MANGROVE SWAMP

Mangrove trees thrive in salty water. Their deep roots help to filter out salt. Many animals shelter in the roots or branches of these trees.

Mangrove branches provide nesting areas for birds like pelicans and spoonbills. Mangrove roots protect nursery areas for fishes, crabs, and shellfish.

ANIMALS IN THIS BOOK

Cuckoo

Leopard Frog

Spoonbill

Green Sea Turtle

Alligator

Mosquito